Wild School

Written by Mairi Mackinnon

Illustrated by Lee Wildish

How this book works

The story of **Wild School** has been written for your child to read with your help. Encourage your child to read as much as they can, helping to sound out the words if they get stuck.

There are puzzles after the story, and for these you will need to read the instructions to your child.

You can find out more about helping your child with this book, and with reading in general, on pages 30-31.

Wild
School

Turn the page to start the story.

"Miss Blair, Miss Blair! There's a hare on my chair."

5

"Can I have a hare?
Miss, it's not fair!"

"Miss Burt, Miss Burt!
See that bird? Is it hurt?"

9

"Miss York, Miss York! There's a hawk on the porch."

15

"Miss Brown, Miss Brown!
There's an owl on
the ground."

19

"Look out, it's Miss Boyd!"

"Now, girls and boys,
And animals too –"

There's TOO
MUCH NOISE!

21

22

23

Puzzle 1

Look at the pictures, read the sentences, then say whether they are true or false.

1.

There's a hare on the stair.

2.

There are four hawks.

3.

Howard found an owl.

4.

Miss Boyd is annoyed.

Puzzle 2

Match the speech bubbles to the pictures.

Puzzle 3

There is one word in each group that **doesn't** rhyme with the rest. Can you spot it?

1. | hare | here | chair | there |

2. | your | our | for | pour |

3. | court | hurt | dirt | shirt |

4. | allow | how | now | slow |

5. | boys | nose | noise | toys |

Answers to puzzles

Puzzle 1

1. False
2. False
3. True
4. True

Puzzle 2

1. "Is it your hawk?" – C
2. "Look, it's pecking my shirt!" – B
3. "Can I have an owl?" – D
4. "Can he share my lunch?" – A

Puzzle 3

1. here
2. our
3. court
4. slow
5. nose

Guidance notes

Usborne Very First Reading is a series of books, specially developed for children who are learning to read. **Wild School** is the eleventh book in the series, and by this stage your child should be able to read the story alone, with occasional help from you.

The story of **Wild School** introduces different spellings of the five sounds shown below:

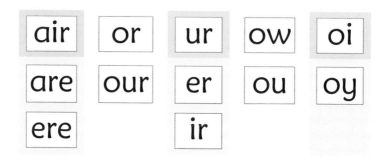

Later books in the series gradually introduce more spelling and pronunciation patterns, while reinforcing the ones your child already knows.

You'll find lots more information about the structure of the series, advice on helping your child with reading, extra practice activities and games on the Very First Reading website,* **www.usborne.com/veryfirstreading**

*US readers go to **www.veryfirstreading.com**

Some questions and answers

- **Why do I need to read with my child?**
  Sharing stories makes reading an enjoyable and fun activity for children. It also helps them to develop confidence and stamina. Even if you are not taking an active part in reading, your listening and support are very important.

- **When is a good time to read?**
  Choose a time when you are both relaxed, but not too tired, and there are no distractions. Only read for as long as your child wants to – you can always try again another day.

- **What if my child gets stuck?**
  Don't simply read the problem word yourself, but prompt your child and try to find the right answer together. Similarly, if your child makes a mistake, go back and look at the word together. Don't forget to give plenty of praise and encouragement.

- **We've finished, now what do we do?**
  It's a good idea to read the story several times to give your child more practice and more confidence. Then, when your child is ready, you can go on to the next book in the series, **The Circus under the Sea.**

Edited by Jenny Tyler and Lesley Sims
Designed by Russell Punter

This edition first published in 2013 by Usborne Publishing Ltd.,
Usborne House, 83-85 Saffron Hill, London EC1N 8RT, England.
www.usborne.com Copyright © 2013, 2010 Usborne Publishing Ltd.